Happy Christmas 2022
Love from

The reception team

Mrs Davoren   Mrs Grava

This Little Tiger book belongs to:

Billie-Mae.

Miss
Sarkis
x

Mrs
Keyser
x

Love from,
Mrs. Fenton
x

Miss Griffin
x

Love from
Ms Stewart
x

For Andy, who sometimes wakes up grumpy
(but mostly lets her sleep) - SS

For Phils . . . play on - CP

LITTLE TIGER PRESS LTD,
an imprint of the Little Tiger Group

1 Coda Studios, 189 Munster Road,
London SW6 6AW
Imported into the EEA by
Penguin Random House Ireland,
Morrison Chambers, 32 Nassau Street,
Dublin D02 YH68
www.littletiger.co.uk

First published in Great Britain 2010
This edition published 2017

ISBN 978-1-84869-754-6

Printed in China
LTP/2700/4241/1121
10 9 8 7 6 5

Don't Wake the Bear, Hare!

Steve Smallman

Caroline Pedler

LITTLE TIGER

LONDON

SPRING PARTY **TODAY** at the old hollow tree

It was Spring Party Day, the best day of the year,
So why were the animals **trembling** with fear?
They'd heard growly noises and crept up to see . . .
A **huge** bear asleep in the old hollow tree!

"Oh no!" they all cried. "But our party's today! How can we get ready with **him** in the way?"

"**I'll wake him up!**" cried a little brown hare.

"No, no!" they all whispered. "Please, don't wake the bear!"

"Bears," Badger said, "are **enormous** and **hairy**.
If you wake them up they get angry and **scary**!
We'll **still** have our party, though, if we take care.
Be quiet as mice so we **don't** wake the bear!"

So they tippy-toed off without making a peep,
To fetch party things while the bear was asleep.
And the ants carried wibbling, wobbling stacks
Of dishes and saucers and cups on their backs.

Badger brought in a huge jelly dessert,
Then he tripped and it fell with a **splat** in the dirt!

zzZZ Z z Z grr humph z Zz z z zᶻ

The bear **stretched** and **grumbled** which gave them a scare.
"**Shh!**" they all whispered. "Please, **don't** wake the bear!"

The lanterns were **carefully** hung in the trees.
The mice **tied up** ribbons that danced on the **breeze**.
They brought in the very last **blueberry** tart
And **their party** was now almost ready to start!

Then Hare cried, "There's only **one** thing left to do!"
And he grabbed a **balloon** and he blew and he blew,

And he **blew** and he **blew** till the others cried, "STOP!
If it gets any **bigger it's going to** - "

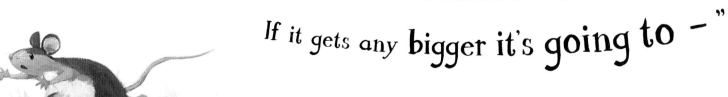

The bear stretched and groaned and they all held their breath,
Then his eyes flickered open and scared them to death!
"Run, run and hide!" they all cried in despair.
"Now we're in trouble, we've woken the bear!"

"WHO DARES WAKE ME UP?"

growled the bear angrily.

Hare said in a small shaky voice.

"It was me!

Our party is going to start very **soon**.

I was trying to **help**, but I popped my balloon . . ."

"A party?" cried Bear, with a grin. "Could it be?
A big surprise party especially for me?

"Oh, **thank you** for waking me up, little bunny. I'll come to your party and bring you some **honey!**"

And even though Bear was enormous and hairy,
They found he was great **fun** and not a bit scary.
He **danced** and he partied with everyone there,
And they all cheered, "Hurray for our new **friend**, the bear!"